Hope
the Happiness
Fairy

Special thanks to Narinder Dhami

ISBN 978-0-545-43390-7

12 11 10 9 8 7 6 5 4 3 2 1   12 13 14 15 16 17/0

Printed in China   68

First Scholastic printing, August 2012

Hope
the Happiness Fairy

by Daisy Meadows

SCHOLASTIC INC.

New York   Toronto   London   Auckland

Sydney   Mexico City   New Delhi   Hong Kong

The Fairyland Palace

The Orangery

The Lake

Maze

Petting Zoo

PETTING ZOO

Garden

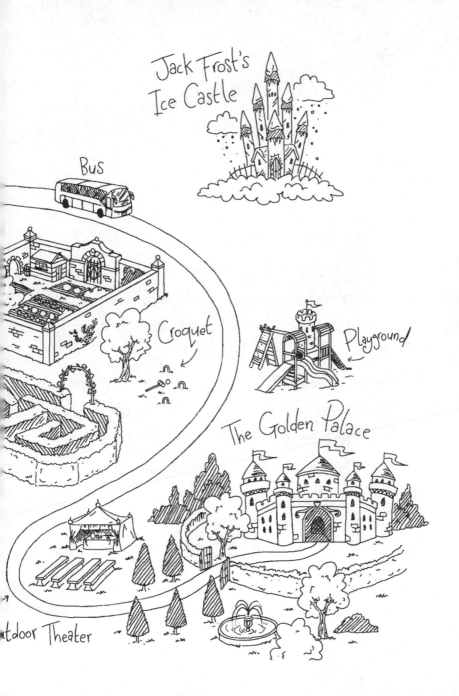

The fairies are planning a magical ball,
With guests of honor and fun for all.
They're expecting a night full of laughter and cheer,
But they'll get a shock when my goblins appear!

Adventures and treats will be things of the past,
And I'll beat those troublesome fairies at last.
My iciest magic will blast through the room
And the world will be plunged into grimness
and gloom!

Contents

Princess Rachel and Princess Kirsty!

"We're here, Kirsty!" Rachel bounced up and down in her seat with excitement as she pointed out the bus window. "Look, that sign says GOLDEN PALACE."

Kirsty beamed at her friend. "I can't believe we get to spend a whole week in a *real* palace." She sighed happily. "I'm beginning to feel like a princess already!"

There were cheers and whoops of joy as the other kids on the bus also noticed the sign. The Golden Palace, a large and beautiful mansion, was located in the country — just outside the village of Wetherbury, where Kirsty lived. The house was always open to the public, but Kirsty had never visited it before. This year, during the week of spring break, the house was holding a special Kids' Royal Sleepover Camp. Kirsty had invited Rachel to come with her.

"I can't wait to see our bedroom," Rachel said eagerly as the bus drove through the tall wrought-iron gates. "Imagine staying in a room that was once used by princes and princesses and other famous visitors!"

"I wonder what activities we're going to be doing this week," Kirsty added. "I hope we get to do lots of princessly things!"

The bus rumbled over a drawbridge and then slowly began to wind its way through the enormous grounds. Like all the other kids on the bus, Rachel and Kirsty stared excitedly out the window. They all strained to catch their first

GOLDEN PALACE

glimpse of the Golden Palace. But there were lots of amazing things on the way to the house that caught their attention, too.

"Look, a petting zoo!" Kirsty exclaimed as they drove past a field of tiny Shetland ponies and little white goats. The girls could see another field with horses and donkeys grazing, and pens of baby piglets, rabbits, and guinea pigs. "The Shetland ponies are so cute!"

"There's a lake over there," Rachel pointed out. The lake was surrounded by beautiful willow trees. Ducks and swans were gliding across the water. "And look at that huge greenhouse, Kirsty. I can see lots of orange and lemon trees growing inside it."

"I think it's called an orangery," Kirsty replied. "I saw one before, when my family visited another country estate."

The bus passed a croquet field with a course of hoops already stuck in the grass. Next, they saw a complicated maze made of tall, close-growing hedges.

"That maze has lots of twists and turns," Rachel whispered to Kirsty. "We might get lost in it and need some fairy magic to find our way out!"

The two girls exchanged a smile. Their friendship with the fairies was a very special secret!

The bus drove through some fancy gardens that were so beautiful, the girls caught their breath in awe. There were huge flowerbeds filled with dazzling colors, fun shapes cut out of hedges, marble statues, fishponds with fountains, and peacocks wandering around. Everyone on the bus, including Rachel and Kirsty, applauded as one of the peacocks spread open his magnificent blue and green tail.

"Here's the Golden Palace, up ahead of us," the bus driver called.

Rachel and Kirsty saw an enormous building made of white stone that gleamed in the sunshine. The palace had four high towers at each corner of the building, and a fifth tower, the highest one, right in the center. The towers were surrounded by golden turrets, and each one had a flag flying on top of it.

"This is so cool, Rachel!" Kirsty breathed, her eyes wide with delight. "I can't wait to explore the palace tomorrow."

"It looks like something out of a fairy tale, doesn't it?" the girl sitting in front of them remarked. Rachel and Kirsty grinned at each other.

"Maybe we'll see some of our fairy friends during our stay here!" Rachel whispered.

The bus came to a stop outside the marble pillars of the palace entrance, and everyone began gathering their things.

As Rachel and Kirsty climbed off the bus with the others, a woman hurried out of the palace, followed by a young man. They both wore stylish navy-blue pantsuits with gold buttons.

"Hi, everyone!" called the woman with a welcoming smile. "I'm Caroline, and this is Louis. We work at the Golden Palace, and we'll be your camp directors during your stay."

"We know you're going to *love* your week here at the Golden Palace," Louis added. "So let's get the fun started right away! The bus driver will bring your bags in while Caroline and I show you around."

Kirsty and Rachel walked through the grand doors, eager like everyone else to get their first glimpse of the inside of the Golden Palace. To their delight, the girls found themselves in a large and very beautiful reception hall. The hall had tall, arched windows, a marble floor, and a high ceiling painted with colorful flowers and birds.

The walls were paneled in rich, dark wood. A giant chandelier hung from the middle of the ceiling and twinkled like diamonds in the sunlight. At the opposite end of the hall, a winding staircase made of pale pink and white marble swept regally to the top floor.

"This is *just* what a palace should be like!" Rachel murmured to Kirsty, who nodded.

"You'll have plenty of time to explore the palace on your own while you're here," Louis said. He waved a hand at the marble stairs. "Now this is called the *grand* staircase!"

he explained. "This is the staircase that the princes and princesses would have used. There's another set of stairs for the servants."

As they all gazed at the impressive staircase, Rachel and Kirsty were interested to see that the walls along the stairs were lined with old portraits in gold frames. "These are pictures of people who used to live or stay in the palace," Caroline told them. "Who's that?" asked Kirsty as she spotted a picture of a girl in a fancy Victorian dress who looked about the same age as her and Rachel.

"That's Princess Charlotte," Caroline replied. "She lived here about one hundred and thirty years ago."

"Caroline and I should warn you that the Golden Palace is full of mysterious secrets," Louis said with a twinkle in his eye. "There are hidden passages, sliding bookcases, secret drawers in the furniture, and all sorts of other amazing things to find!" He pushed one corner of the wooden panel closest to him. Everyone gasped in astonishment as a whole length of paneling moved aside, revealing a dark passageway behind it.

"This is going to be such an adventure!" Rachel said to

Kirsty. "*And* we get to be princesses for a week!"

"You're allowed to go pretty much wherever you want in the palace," Louis explained, "except for the highest tower. The staircase stones are loose, so it's not safe."

"It's time for dinner," Caroline announced, leading the way down the hall. "After you eat, we'll take you to your rooms and you can settle in for the night."

After a dinner of grilled cheese and mugs of creamy hot chocolate in the majestic banquet hall, Caroline took Rachel and Kirsty to their bedroom. It was beautifully decorated in shades of blue and gold, and it had twin four-poster beds with matching bedspreads printed with a pattern of peacock feathers. A silver and glass chandelier hung from the ceiling, shimmering in the light.

"See you tomorrow, girls," Caroline called as she closed the door behind her.

"Isn't this gorgeous?" Rachel said, gazing at the antique beds. "It's just like being real princesses! I guess we should unpack before we go to sleep, Kirsty."

"Do princesses do their own unpacking?" Kirsty asked with a grin. She glanced up to admire the chandelier—and the smile disappeared from her face. She frowned, confused. "Rachel, I'm sure that chandelier has gotten much brighter since we came in!"

Rachel also gazed upward. "You're right, Kirsty," she exclaimed, shading her eyes. "It's so bright now, I can hardly look at it!"

At that moment, a tiny sparkling figure spun out of the middle of the shimmering chandelier and danced through the air toward them.

"It's a fairy, Rachel!" Kirsty gasped. "And we know her—it's Polly the Party Fun Fairy!"

Enter the
Princess Fairies

"Yes, it's me, girls!" Polly zoomed down toward them, her long red curls flowing behind her. She beamed at Rachel and Kirsty. "King Oberon and Queen Titania asked me to bring you a *very* special invitation. Would you like to come to a Fairyland ball?"

The girls looked thrilled.

"Of course we would!" Rachel cried.

"That's the answer I was hoping for."
Polly laughed. "Get ready—we're off to
Fairyland. One, two, three!"

Polly flicked her wand in the air, and
showers of glittering fairy dust swirled
around the girls. Instantly,
Rachel and Kirsty
felt themselves spinning
through the air as
Polly's magic carried
them to Fairyland.
Just a few seconds
later, Rachel, Kirsty,
and Polly arrived outside
the Fairyland Palace in the shadow of
its golden towers. The girls were
delighted to see that all their fairy friends
were waiting there, along with the king
and queen.

"Welcome, Rachel and Kirsty!" King Oberon announced with a smile.

"We're so glad you could join us for this very special ball, girls," Queen Titania added. The other fairies clapped and cheered. "Thank you for coming."

"Thank you for inviting us!" said Kirsty.

"But why is it a very *special* ball, Your Majesty?" Rachel asked.

"Because we're waiting for some *very* honored guests," the queen explained. "The seven Princess Fairies should be here any moment now!"

"The Princess Fairies are

our cousins," King Oberon explained.
"They live far away in a distant land."

Suddenly the *clip-clop* of horses' hooves
could be heard in the distance.

"That must be the Princess Fairies'
carriage!" the queen exclaimed.
"Where's Bertram?"

Bertram the frog
footman hopped
forward. "Here,
Your Majesty."

"All the footmen
must be ready to receive
the princesses," the queen told him.
Rachel and Kirsty glanced around and
saw a group of footmen standing nearby
in the background, their hats pulled
down over their faces.

A glass carriage drawn by two snow-white horses was now approaching the palace. As Rachel and Kirsty watched, the carriage came to a stop and Bertram sprang forward to open the door. He helped the Princess Fairies out one by one as the watching crowd applauded loudly.

"Aren't their ball gowns gorgeous?" Kirsty whispered to Rachel. "And look at their tiaras!" Rachel whispered back. "They're so sparkly, and each one has a different jewel in the center."

"Welcome, Princess Fairies!" Queen Titania announced. "It's wonderful to see you all again."

"Please follow us to the royal ballroom," King Oberon announced, "and let the ball begin!"

The king and queen led the way to the ballroom, with Polly the Party Fun Fairy, Rachel, and Kirsty following closely behind them.

Bertram escorted the Princess Fairies to the ballroom. Meanwhile, the other footmen were left to take care of the horses and the glass carriage.

"Oh, this is magical!" Rachel gasped as Polly showed them into the ballroom. The pink and gold room was lit with candles and decorated with garlands of

sweetly scented white flowers. A fairy
band—made up of the girls' friends the
Music Fairies—was filling the air with
music.

"Now we shall give the Princess Fairies
a proper introduction," Queen Titania

said to Rachel and Kirsty as all the
fairies gathered around. "They're
wearing beautiful
ball gowns for this
special occasion,
instead of their
regular fairy
outfits!"

Bertram led
the first Princess
Fairy into the
ballroom.

"Welcome,
Princess Hope
the Happiness
Fairy!" the queen
announced.

Rachel and Kirsty and all the other
fairies curtsied as Princess Hope waved

and smiled. She wore a white gown with crystal embroidery. A sparkling tiara set with a ruby glistened against her dark hair. The queen then introduced Princess Cassidy the Costume Fairy, Princess Anya the Cuddly Creatures Fairy, Princess Elisa the Royal Adventure Fairy, Princess Lizzie the Sweet Treats Fairy, Princess Maddie the Fun and Games

Fairy, and Princess Eva the Enchanted Ballet Fairy.

Everyone broke into loud applause.

All of a sudden, a freezing blast of icy wind swept through the ballroom, making everyone shiver. The music crashed to a halt and all the candles went out.

"Beware, everyone!" shouted King Oberon, holding on to his crown as the frozen wind swirled around and icicles formed on the chandeliers. "This is one of Jack Frost's magical ice bolts!" Rachel and Kirsty glanced at each other in dismay. They were even more horri~~ when they noticed that all the Princess Fairies' beautiful ball gowns had turned to tattered rags. At that moment, the ballroom doors flew open. Jack Frost and a pair of goblins strolled in, wearing footman disguises.

"Surprise!" sneered Jack Frost, throwing his hat to the floor.

Tiara Thieves!

Rachel, Kirsty, and everyone in the ballroom ducked as Jack Frost raised his wand. He sent another ice bolt spinning toward them! The Princess Fairies cried out in shock as their glittering tiaras were whipped off their heads. In an instant, the tiaras flew through the air and landed on the heads of the goblins.

Jack Frost roared with laughter as the goblins looked very smug and began primping. "Who's a pretty princess now?" cackled one goblin. "WE ARE!" the others chorused proudly. "Please give our tiaras back," Princess Hope pleaded.

"Oh, this isn't good!" Princess Anya exclaimed. "We Princess Fairies are responsible for *all* fairy magic. Without our tiaras, no human or fairy will ever have a happy or magical time again!"

"Good," Jack Frost snorted. "I want everyone to be miserable! We're going to hide the tiaras in the human world, and you Princess Fairies will never see your magic tiaras again—ha, ha, ha!" Lifting his wand, he fired a third ice bolt straight at the goblins.

But Rachel and Kirsty saw Queen Titania point her own wand at the goblins, too. A magical bolt of pink and purple mist shot toward them just as Jack Frost and the goblins disappeared with shouts of triumph.

"I wasn't able to stop them from disappearing to the human world," Queen Titania explained. "But my magic has made sure that they will all end up at the Golden Palace!"

Rachel and Kirsty noticed that the queen's magic had made the Princess Fairies' ragged ball gowns vanish, too. Each of them was now wearing a new outfit.

"Girls, we will need your help once again to get the Princess Fairies' tiaras back," the queen went on. "All fairy magic depends on it!"

"We'll do our best," Kirsty promised, and Rachel nodded in agreement. All of the fairies looked relieved.

"The Princess Fairies will help you in your search," King Oberon told them. "But first, you girls should go back and get a good night's sleep."

"Good night, Rachel and Kirsty. We'll see you again soon!" the fairies called as another wave of the queen's wand sent the two girls zooming off to the Golden Palace.

Back in their bedroom, Rachel and Kirsty quickly unpacked and got ready for bed. "Can you believe the nerve of Jack Frost, crashing the fairies' ball?" Kirsty said sleepily as she snuggled under the covers.

"Well, we'll be ready to stop his plans tomorrow!" Rachel replied with a yawn.

But when Rachel woke up the next morning, she still felt very tired.

"I didn't get a good night's sleep at all!" she said grumpily to Kirsty. "This mattress is really lumpy. I wonder if there's something hidden underneath it, like in 'The Princess and the Pea.'"

Kirsty sat up and began scratching her

arms. "My quilt is really itchy," she grumbled. "I wish it wasn't, because I'm so grouchy—I feel like hiding underneath it all day!"

The girls still hadn't cheered up by the time they'd brushed their teeth, dressed, and gone down to breakfast.

Meals at the Golden Palace were served on long wooden tables covered with white cloths in the banquet hall. The whole room was decorated with beautiful tapestries. But this morning, no one looked as if they were enjoying themselves at all.

"I don't *want* a royal breakfast of biscuits and bacon," one boy said, sulking. "I just want my favorite cereal!"

"My orange juice isn't sweet enough!" another girl complained. "And these biscuits have too much butter."

"Oh, Kirsty, I just realized what's happening!" Rachel murmured in her friend's ear. "Everyone's miserable because Hope the Happiness Fairy lost her tiara!"

Kirsty nodded. "Let's hope we find it soon," she replied. "Otherwise everyone's vaation at the Golden Palace is going to be ruined!"

After breakfast, Louis and Caroline took them all into the library. It was a magnificent room filled with huge bookcases of leather-bound books, but everyone still looked very glum.

"OK, we thought we'd act out some prince and princess stories," Caroline said, trying to sound cheerful. "We'll start with 'Cinderella'! That'll be fun, won't it?"

No one said anything.

"And we even have some pretend glass slippers, too!" Louis pulled a pair of high-heeled shoes out of a nearby cabinet and held them up on a cushion.

Caroline gave the kids different parts to play, even though none of them were very enthusiastic. Rachel and Kirsty were guests at the prince's ball, and they watched as the girl playing Cinderella ran off at the stroke of midnight, leaving her glass slipper behind. But when the boy playing the prince asked everyone to try on the glass slipper, it didn't fit anyone—not even Cinderella!

"I don't understand," complained Cinderella, trying to force her foot into the shoe. "It fit just a little while ago!"

"Everything's going wrong," the prince

said sadly. "This isn't the right ending to the story."

"Yes, and we know why!" Kirsty whispered in Rachel's ear.

"OK, maybe we should try something else," Louis suggested, glancing anxiously at Caroline. "Why don't you get into pairs and write your own stories?"

"It's a nice sunny day, so go and explore the gardens for inspiration," Caroline said as she and Louis handed out velvet-covered notebooks and gold pens. "We'll all meet up later to share our stories."

Rachel and Kirsty left the library and

headed toward the gardens along with everyone else. But as they passed the grand staircase, Kirsty grabbed Rachel's arm.

"Rachel, look at the portrait of Princess Charlotte," Kirsty said in a low voice. "There's a golden light shining from behind it!"

As everyone else went outside, the girls stayed back, gazing up at the bright light. Then a fairy fluttered out from behind the painting and danced through the air toward them!

"It's me, girls!" called Princess Hope the Happiness Fairy, "I'm here to search for my magical tiara. Will you help me?"

"Of course we will!" Rachel and Kirsty cried.

Green
Fingers!

"Thank you, girls," Hope said gratefully. She now wore a beautiful red shift dress with a large bow on the front, and gold sandals. "Where do you think we should start looking?"

"We're supposed to be going out to the gardens," Kirsty told her, "so maybe we should start there."

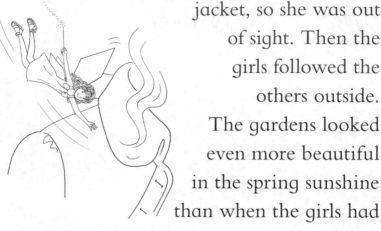

Hope nodded. She flew down and
slipped under the collar of Rachel's
jacket, so she was out
of sight. Then the
girls followed the
others outside.
The gardens looked
even more beautiful
in the spring sunshine
than when the girls had
seen them from the bus the day before.
Daffodils and tulips nodded their heads
in the warm breeze, and the marble
fountains sent sparkling sprays of water
into the air. But Rachel and Kirsty still
didn't feel like smiling. Neither did any
of the other kids, who were wandering
around the lush green lawns looking
grumpy.

"See that peacock?" said Kirsty, pointing out the bird to Rachel. The peacock walked down one of the gravel paths, its tail feathers firmly closed and drooping on the ground. "He looks exactly how I feel!"

"Oh, dear," Hope murmured, sounding distressed. "Everyone should be having a wonderful time here at the Golden Palace. We *must* find my tiara, girls!"

Keeping a sharp eye out for the missing tiara, Rachel and Kirsty went over to join some of the other kids. They were staring at the figures that the gardeners had clipped out of the thick leafy hedges.

"Look, there's a prince and a princess," Rachel said, pointing at two green figures with crowns on their heads. The prince and the princess appeared to be dancing. "And there's a teddy bear, too!"

"This one is a witch," Kirsty added, admiring a very complicated figure in a pointed hat sitting on her broomstick. "Rachel, maybe these characters would be good for our story?"

Rachel nodded. "Let's see what others there are," she suggested. "Look, there are some gardeners working on new figures on the other side of that hedge."

The group of gardeners was clipping away at the branches of the hedge, concentrating on the shape they were making. Rachel and Kirsty went to look. Along the way, they peered under all the hedges to see if they could spot the tell-tale magical sparkle of Hope's missing tiara. But there was nothing.

The gardeners had on sun hats with large brims that covered their faces. Rachel also noticed that they had very big feet. She began to look at them suspiciously.

Then one of the gardeners pulled off his gardening glove, tilted back the brim of his hat, and scratched his long green nose with his finger.

"These gardeners have green thumbs *and* green fingers!" Kirsty exclaimed. "They're goblins in disguise!"

"And look," Hope whispered. "They're trimming the hedge into the shape of Jack Frost holding his ice wand!"

As Hope and the girls watched, the goblins finished sculpting Jack Frost's head and stood back proudly to admire their work. Quickly, Rachel and Kirsty ducked behind the hedge on the other side.

"I wonder if they have the tiara with them," Kirsty said in a low voice.

"Let's listen to their conversation and find out!" Hope suggested. "It'll be easier to stay out of sight if I turn you both into fairies."

Rachel and Kirsty nodded. A few swishes of Hope's wand sent a stream of fairy sparkles whirling around them. The girls instantly shrank down until they were exactly the same size as Hope, with the same glittery wings. Then the three friends fluttered out from behind the

hedge. Quietly, Hope led them over to the figure of Jack Frost. The goblins had moved on to a new part of the hedge, and were discussing what shape to make next. Putting her finger to her lips, Hope landed silently on the branch that formed Jack Frost's icicle beard. Rachel and Kirsty joined her.

"Let's make this part of the hedge into the shape of Jack Frost's Ice Castle," suggested one of the goblins with a grin.

A second goblin nodded. "This is much more fun than that silly maze we got lost in," he remarked.

"Yes, but it was a good idea to hide that magical tiara in the middle of the maze, wasn't it?" the first goblin replied. "Those pesky fairies will never find it there! Ha, ha!"

Into the Maze

Hope, Rachel, and Kirsty glanced at one another in delight. The tiara was hidden in the maze!

"It was *my* idea to put it there," boasted the second goblin.

"No, I was the one who thought of it!" snapped a third goblin.

Leaving the goblins squabbling as they clipped away at the hedge, Hope, Rachel, and Kirsty zoomed off toward the maze. Luckily, it was close to the garden.

"It will be easy to spot the middle of the maze from above," Hope said as they flew over the twisting and turning rows of thick hedges. "We won't get lost, girls!"

But as Hope and the girls neared the center of the maze, they heard the sound of gruff voices.

"That sounds like more goblins!" Kirsty whispered, making a face.

"They must have stayed behind to guard the tiara," said Rachel.

Hope and the girls quickly swooped down toward the middle of the maze and hid in a thick patch of leaves. They peeked out and immediately spotted two goblins. One of them was posing with Hope's beautiful tiara on his head, while the other was doing his best to sculpt a

figure of himself in the hedge, with the tiara on top. Rachel, Kirsty, and Hope tried not to give themselves away by laughing.

As the second goblin finished his figure, the goblin wearing the tiara rushed forward to take a closer look. He was now standing very close to where Rachel was hidden in the hedge.

"You made my nose too big!" the tiara-wearing goblin grumbled.

"No, I didn't," the other insisted. "It *is* big — it's huge!"

Rachel saw her chance. She flew out of the hedge! Hovering in the air, she reached down to lift the tiara from the goblin's head. But to Rachel's dismay, the other goblin spotted her.

"Pesky fairy!" he snapped, glaring at Rachel. Then he turned to his friend. "Run for it!" he shouted.

As Hope and Kirsty flew out of the hedge to join Rachel, the goblins took off running. One went left and one went right.

"Fly after the one who has the tiara!" Hope told Rachel and Kirsty. But when the goblin saw that they were following him, he took the tiara off.

"Catch!" he roared, and threw it over the hedge to the goblin who was running on the other side.

Hope, Rachel, and Kirsty flew over to him, but the goblin immediately tossed the tiara under the hedge, back to the first one.

"This is impossible!" Rachel panted as the goblins continued to race around the maze, flinging the tiara from one to the other as if it were a ball. "How are we going to get the tiara back?"

Kirsty made a grab for the tiara as one of the goblins tossed it over a hedge, but it sailed right past her. With a smug chuckle, the other goblin grabbed it and ran off.

"Can't catch me!" he boasted, waving the tiara around.

Kirsty glanced desperately around for inspiration. Her gaze fell on the goblin figure made from the hedge.

"Oh!" she exclaimed. "I have an idea!"

Happy Days Are Here Again

Kirsty whispered her plan to Hope and Rachel, who smiled and nodded.

"We'll have to distract the goblins, Rachel, while Hope works her magic!" Kirsty told her friend.

The girls flew after the goblins, drawing them away from the center of the maze. Kirsty glanced back over her

shoulder and saw Hope point her wand
at the hedge goblin. A magical mist of
fairy dust surrounded it, and right away

the goblin made of
leaves and twigs
turned into a
real goblin!
"Everything's going
according to plan,"
Kirsty whispered,
delighted.
"Hey, you two!"
a gruff voice called to the goblins. Kirsty
and Rachel exchanged a hopeful glance
as the goblins spun around. The girls
knew that Hope was using her magic to
make her voice sound just like a goblin!
"Throw the tiara to me right away—or
those pesky fairies will get it!"

"Here, take it!" shouted the goblin
with the tiara, hurling it through the air.

The hedge goblin easily caught the
tiara, but as he did, he began to turn
back to leaves and
twigs again.
Kirsty and
Rachel flew
forward and
caught the tiara
before it fell to the
ground. Then Hope
fluttered out to join them.
The two goblins groaned loudly as they
realized that they'd been tricked.

"What's Jack Frost going to say?"
one of them mumbled angrily as they
stomped away.

"And how are we going to find our

way out of this maze?" the other goblin
wanted to know.

Kirsty and Rachel passed
the tiara to Hope. As
soon as she touched
it, the tiara shrank
down to its fairy size,
and Hope placed
it carefully on her
head. Rachel and Kirsty smiled.
"My magic is working already!" Hope
laughed. "That's the first time I've seen
you smile all day, girls! And now
everyone else will be happy, too. Thank
you for your help. Now I must rush back
to Fairyland and tell my princess sisters
the great news! I know they'll be hoping
that you'll help them find their tiaras,
too."

"We'll do our best," Rachel promised as Hope fluttered off to Fairyland in a shower of rainbow-colored fairy magic.

"We'd better go back to the library with everyone else," said Kirsty as they saw the other kids making their way back into the Golden Palace. As the girls hurried to join them, they saw that everyone was now chatting happily, smiling and laughing and obviously enjoying themselves.

"What a difference!" Rachel whispered to Kirsty.

Caroline and Louis were waiting in the

library for them, and everyone settled down to write their stories.

"Let's write something really magical," Kirsty suggested. "We could have the princess from the portrait by the grand staircase as our heroine."

"Good idea," Rachel agreed, beginning to write.

After a little while, Louis suggested that they share their stories. "Rachel and Kirsty, would you like to go first?"

The girls stood up and, taking turns, they read their story out loud. It was about a princess named Charlotte who was sad because she'd lost her smile. But with the help of a talking peacock and a teddy bear cut from a hedge, she found it hidden in the middle of the maze. Everyone listened in silence, and when

Rachel and Kirsty finished, there was a round of applause.

"What a wonderful, magical story," Caroline said. "Nice work."

"There's something about the Golden Palace that almost makes you believe in magic!" said one of the girls, and Rachel and Kirsty grinned at each other.

"So, has everyone had a happy first day at the Golden Palace?" asked Louis.

Everyone shouted "YES!"

"And we have another exciting adventure with the Princess Fairies to look forward to tomorrow!" Kirsty murmured to Rachel.

Rachel and Kirsty have helped
Hope find her tiara.
Now it's time for them to help

Cassidy
the Costume Fairy!

Join their next adventure
in this special sneak peek. . . .

Cool
Jewels

Kirsty and Rachel walked along the
stone hallway with a group of kids.
They were all chatting excitedly. It
was the second day of their stay at the
Golden Palace, a beautiful mansion
in the countryside. They were having
a wonderful time! The Golden Palace
was amazing—it had been built from
gleaming white stone hundreds of years

ago, and had high towers topped with golden turrets. The owners of the palace were having a special Kids' Royal Sleepover Camp during spring break. It included lots of different fun activities.

Yesterday, the girls had found themselves on a brand-new fairy adventure! This time, they were helping the Princess Fairies look for their magical tiaras. The Princess Fairies were cousins of the king and queen of Fairyland. They had been their special guests at a Fairyland Palace ball, but naughty Jack Frost and his mischievous goblins had snuck into the ball—and had stolen the seven Princess Fairies' tiaras. The tiaras were full of powerful fairy magic. Without them, no human or fairy could have a happy or magical time!

"Follow me, everyone. Come and see the palace's Jewel Chamber," said Louis, one of the palace directors who was running the camp. "Through here."

Kirsty and Rachel followed the group into a small wood-paneled room that had glass display cases along the walls. "Wow," Kirsty breathed, as she stared into the first case. "Princess Charlotte's christening bracelet from when she was a baby—a gift from the Spanish royal family, over two hundred years ago!"

RAINBOW magic™

There's Magic in Every Series!

The Rainbow Fairies
The Weather Fairies
The Jewel Fairies
The Pet Fairies
The Fun Day Fairies
The Petal Fairies
The Dance Fairies
The Music Fairies
The Sports Fairies
The Party Fairies
The Ocean Fairies
The Night Fairies
The Magical Animal Fairies
The Princess Fairies

Read them all!

■ SCHOLASTIC

www.scholastic.com
www.rainbowmagiconline.com

RMFAIRY6